Mermaid Treasure

Written by Lisa Thompson
Pictures by Craig Smith and Lew Keilar

Bones, the sea dog, was up on the lookout. "Mermaid ahead!" he called.

"Shiver me timbers!" said Captain Red Beard. He grabbed his telescope. "The mermaid is inviting us over."

Captain Red Beard knew it was bad luck to say no to a mermaid.

"Thank you for stopping," said the mermaid. "I'm moving into a new cave, but my mermaid treasure chest is stuck in the rocks. Would you help me to get it out?"

"Did you say treasure?" asked Lizzie, the first mate.

4

Captain Red Beard took a long, careful look. He knew it was bad luck to say no to a mermaid.

"Pesky Pirates!" said Fingers, the parrot.

Captain Red Beard asked the mermaid to tie a rope around her treasure chest. The crew grabbed the other end of the rope.

"Heave-ho," said Captain Red Beard. The crew pulled and pulled.

The treasure chest squeaked and moaned, but it did not budge. It was still stuck in the rocks.

The Captain joined the crew at the end of the rope. "Heave-ho!" said the Captain again.

The mermaid's treasure chest flew out from between the rocks. It hit another rock and burst open. Hundreds of pieces of seaweed scattered everywhere.

"What a mess," said Bones, the sea dog.

The mermaid was unhappy. "My seaweed treasure!" she cried.

"Seaweed treasure?" said Captain Red Beard. He wanted to laugh.

"You must help me collect it all," said the mermaid.

The Captain knew it was bad luck to say no to a mermaid.

"Lower the boat. We must help the mermaid collect her seaweed," said the Captain.

They collected every last bit of seaweed treasure.

"Thank you so much," said the mermaid. "I don't know what I would do without my treasure. Could you do one more thing for me before you leave?"

"Yes," said the Captain.

"My new cave is full of junk.
Could you take it with you?" she asked.

The Captain was happy he had said
yes to the mermaid!

What was strange about the mermaid's treasure?

How did the pirates feel when they had to help the mermaid?

How did the Captain feel at the end of the story, and why?